The Great Smoky Mountain Salamander Ball

by Lisa Horstman

©1997 Great Smoky Mountains Association
Story, illustration, and design by Lisa Horstman
Edited by Karen Ballentine, Don DeFoe, and Steve Kemp
Project Coordination by Steve Kemp
Environmental Education advice by
Dr. Ruth Wilson and Ken Voorhis
Printed in China 15 16 17 18 19 20
ISBN 0-937207-21-7
Published by Great Smoky Mountains Association,
a nonprofit organization assisting Great Smoky Mountains
National Park since 1953.
P.O. Box 130, Gatlinburg, TN 37738.
(865) 436-7318   www.SmokiesInformation.org
All purchases benefit the park.

About the author

Lisa Horstman lives and works in Knoxville, Tennessee, in sight of the Great Smoky Mountains. This is her second children's book. Her first, *Fast Friends*, won the prestigious Dr. Seuss Picture Book Award. She is a member of The Authors Guild, Inc., and The Authors League of America, Inc.

This book is for Dave.—*LH*

On top of the car roof the camp gear was stacked.
And into the car with their suitcases packed
Went both Sara's parents, with Sara there too.
They had places to go! They had fun things to do!

Sara wriggled and squiggled inside the big car
And asked, "Are we there yet?" because it seemed far.
They were bound for the Smokies, that wonderful spot
Where hikes would be hiked and fish would be caught.

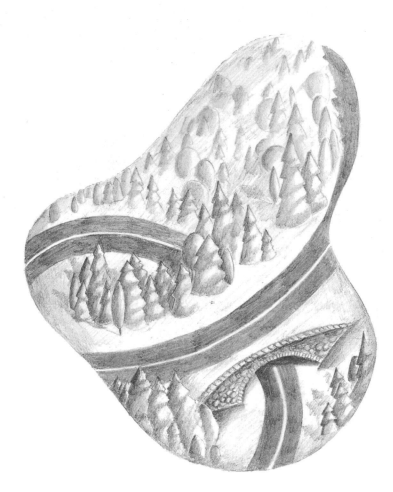

Once in the Smokies, the days went by fast
With hiking and swimming and fishing lines cast.
Sara learned lots about mountains and trees,
Why some trees have needles, why some trees have leaves.

The mountains and Sara were no longer strangers.
She'd joined the ranks of the park's Junior Rangers.
She'd worked hard to earn a nice shiny badge
Awarded to her by Park Ranger Madge.

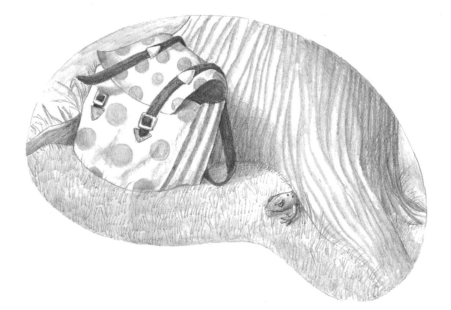

Picking up litter had been quite a chore.
Hiking was tough, though she liked to explore.
But she knew of one kid who'd cheated and lied.
He bragged about hiking he'd not even tried.

And that isn't all—there was more, Sara knew.
He's not just a liar, but a big bully, too.
He'd yanked off the tail of a little red newt
Before it escaped and hid under a root.

Then came the night Sara just couldn't sleep.
Dreams wouldn't come so she tried counting sheep
'Til she heard a strange noise and peeked from her tent,
And sneaked through the darkness with no one's consent.

Poking through trees, she came to a hollow.
She saw teeny footprints and started to follow.
Crunch! She looked down—a small piece of paper!
There in the dark it had almost escaped her.

It seemed to be some kind of fine invitation
Of which Sara studied with great fascination.
She held it up close to the eyes in her head
And started to read it—here's what it said:

To Salamanders big!
To Salamanders small!
Come one, come all
to the Salamander Ball.
We'll have a big party. Yes,
this much is true,
with feasting and dancing
and playing games, too.

SALAMANDER BALL

Then what she saw, she couldn't resist,
She just had to follow, for there in the mist
Salamanders busily heeded the call
To where she now knew—the Salamander Ball.

They all reached a clearing on top of a mountain
And someone yelled loudly, "A ball's to be startin'!"
A small band of crickets then started to play
As the guests wandered in on a fancy pathway.

First a Hellbender marched in
with great zest
With plans to win big
in the "Ugly Contest."

Next came a Pigmy,
the smallest of small.
He took a high place—
it made him look tall.

The Zigzag Salamanders all zigzagged in time
To the beat of a drummer while standing in line.

Behind them the red cheeks swayed to the band,
Admiring their blushes to see whose was grand.

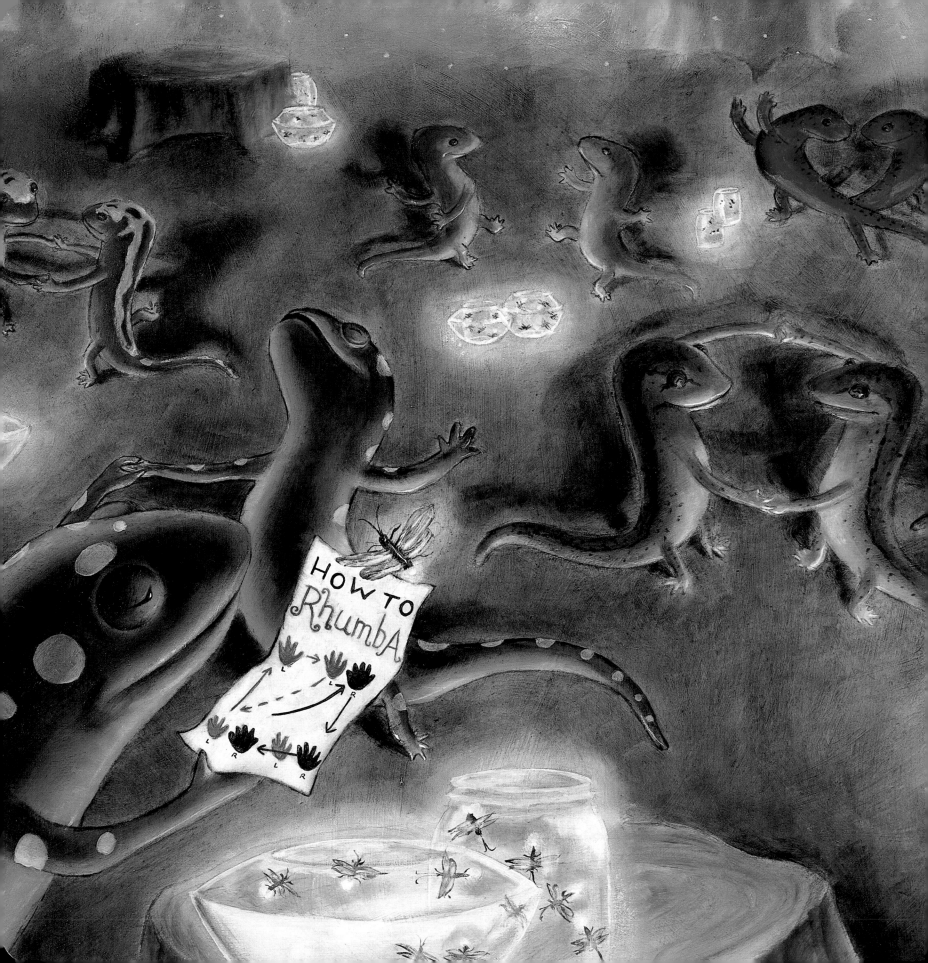

The Mud Salamander bathed just for the occasion
And found a dance partner without much persuasion.
On went the dancing; they all kept time well.
They rhumba'd and cha-cha'd and polka'd pell-mell.

They'd moved up the mountain in pack after pack,
Now there were so many that Sara lost track.
So many colors and so many sizes,
So many talents; all hoping for prizes.

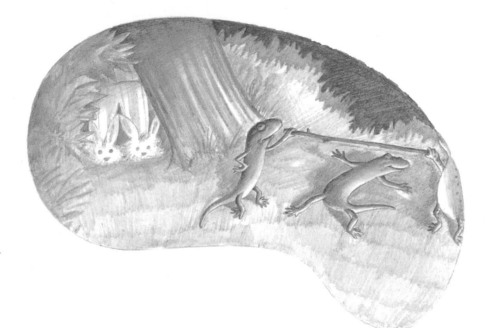

Laughing and watching from her hiding spot,
Sara saw weird things—until she got caught.
Two alert newts called out, "It's a spy!"
Sara stopped laughing and tried not to cry.

Everyone froze—this was not a good thing.
The Salamander Ball was a top-secret fling.
They circled around her and grumbled and glared.
They all moved in closer and Sara got scared.

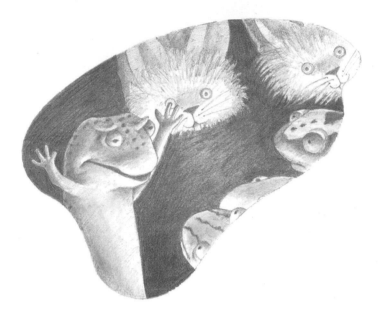

"What to do now?" yelled a voice above all,
"No human has been to our Salamander Ball.
It's ruined for sure. Forget having more.
The Ball would be crowded with Humans galore."

Sara was sorry that she'd spoiled their fun,
And just when their party had barely begun.
But then someone called amid the uproar,
"Let's make this girl an Ambassador!"

"What's that?" they all muttered, craning their heads
As up stepped Simon, blushing bright red.
He was a true leader, somewhat of a brain.
They all stopped to listen; he began to explain.

"Ambassadors help us to see wrong from right,
They help keep the peace instead of a fight.
She'd be the one to teach the human race
To respect salamanders—and our Smoky Mountain place."

They all stared at Sara, and what could she do?
Ambassador she'd be—and a diplomat, too.
So now it was time for some grand lecturing
On Two Golden Rules of Salamandering.

"Rule Number One," began Simon right off,
"Put back that salamander before you take off.
His home's in the Smokies and not home with you.
He's happiest here and the weather's right, too."

"And Rule Number Two should never be broken,
One to be remembered long after I've spoken.
The Great Smoky Mountains
have been home since creation,
So please treat them kindly
when you're here on vacation."

They gave her a ribbon that made her proud-hearted,
The music began and the party restarted.

A race for the fastest
began with a shout,

And a prize for the best
spots was then given out.

Near one clump of trees
a scary movie was shown
Of a salamander chased
by a boy just half-grown.
That kid was just curious
and needed to know—
If a tail gets yanked off,
will another one grow?

Then trumpets blasted; a pageant took place
To decide which contestant was fairest of face.
Not to be missed was a fine diving show
Making all in the crowd shout "Magnifico!"

The party went onward throughout the dark night,
And Sara fought sleep off, but try as she might
Her eyes soon grew heavy; she dropped off to sleep
And went off to dreamland without counting sheep.

Just think if this story had happened to you—
Was it simply a dream, or was it all true?
Well, Sara grew up, and now she's a ranger.
She protects salamanders from possible danger.

So maybe she dreamed it, but then maybe not,
What matters the most is what she was taught.
And maybe, just maybe, if you make a request,
She'll tell you about that salamander fest.

And if Sara likes you, she'll show you the badge
Awarded to her by Park Ranger Madge.
But look very closely, there's a little bit more—
A ribbon attached reads "AMBASSADOR."

Have You Seen us?

Types of salamanders you can find in the Great Smoky Mountains National Park.

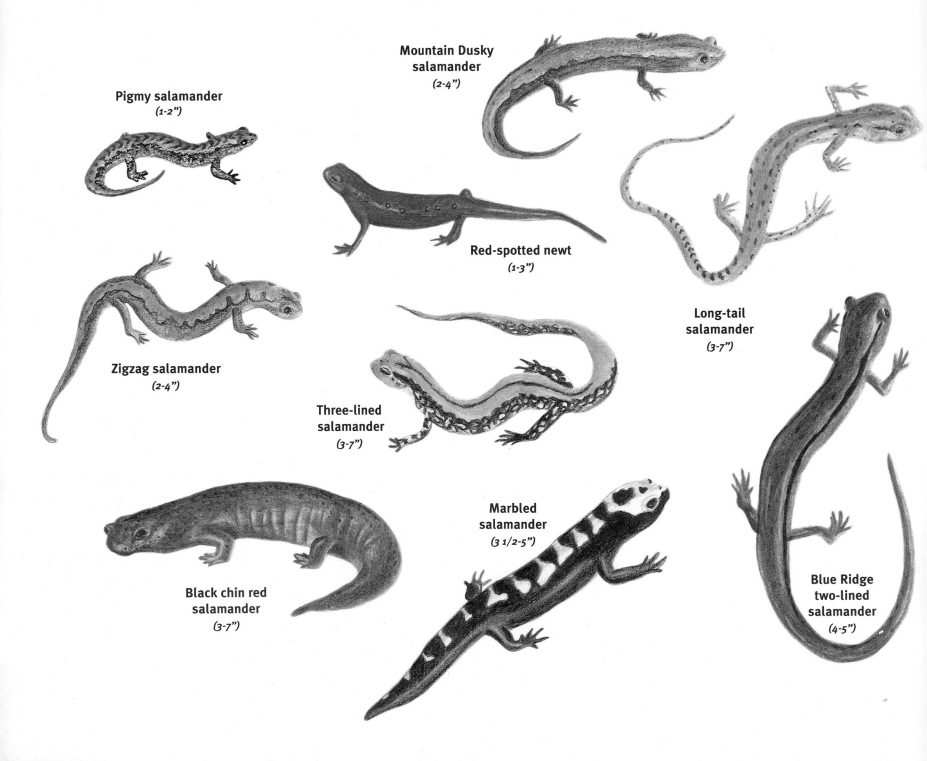

Mountain Dusky salamander *(2-4")*

Pigmy salamander *(1-2")*

Red-spotted newt *(1-3")*

Long-tail salamander *(3-7")*

Zigzag salamander *(2-4")*

Three-lined salamander *(3-7")*

Black chin red salamander *(3-7")*

Marbled salamander *(3 1/2-5")*

Blue Ridge two-lined salamander *(4-5")*